ALIEN INVASION

LEVEL UP

ALIEN INVASION

ISRAEL KEATS

darbycreek

MINNEAPOLIS

Darby Creek
A division of Lerner Publishing Group, Inc.
241 First Avenue North
Minneapolis, MN 55401 USA

For reading levels and more information, look up this title at
www.lernerbooks.com.

Images in this book used with the permission of: © medvesky.kz/Shutterstock.com (spaceship interior), © Maria Starovoytova/Shutterstock.com (space background), © iStockphoto.com/Thoth_Adan (grunge background).

Main body text set in Janson Text LT Std 12/17.5.
Typeface provided by Adobe Systems.

Library of Congress Cataloging-in-Publication Data

The Cataloging-in-Publication Data for *Alien Invasion* is on file at the Library of Congress.
ISBN 978-1-5124-3984-7 (lib. bdg.)
ISBN 978-1-5124-5356-0 (pbk.)
ISBN 978-1-5124-4873-3 (EB pdf)

Manufactured in the United States of America
1-42233-25782-2/17/2017

To Isaac Asimov

It is the year 2089. Virtual reality games are part of everyday life, and one company—L33T CORP—is behind the most popular games. Though most people are familiar with L33T CORP, few know much about what happens behind the scenes of the megacorporation.

L33T CORP has developed a new virtual reality game: *Level Up*. It contains more than one thousand unique virtual realities for gamers to play. But the company needs testers to smooth out glitches. Teenagers from around the country are chosen for this task and, suddenly, they find themselves in the middle of a video game. The company gives them a warning—win the game, or be trapped within it. Forever.

CHAPTER 1

The gamer didn't know what kind of game he would get.

Anything is fine, as long as it's not boring, he thought to himself. *I want lots to explore. Secrets to discover and loot to find.*

He found himself on a platform in outer space, surrounded by stars. The L33T C0RP logo glowed under his feet. He reached out and touched something solid and clear, like glass, but totally invisible. Clearly he was on some kind of enclosed observation deck. He looked out at the distant stars.

Wonder if I'll get to fly around out there. That would be cool.

"Sorry I kept you waiting," a voice said from behind him. He turned around and saw a tall man in a white suit and sunglasses.

"It's fine," the gamer replied. "I like looking at the stars. Although my teachers call it staring off into space." He snorted at his own joke, but the man didn't even smile.

"You can call me the Game Runner," he said. "I'm here to debrief you about the game."

"I can see it's set in outer space," the gamer said.

"Yes, it is. In this game, you are a member of a small crew of space explorers who have been captured by a hostile Orionan crew—"

"Because they're from Orion?"

"Exactly. We're in a three-star system that's part of the Orion constellation." As the Game Runner went on explaining the game, the gamer got restless.

He shifted his weight from one foot to the other. *When do I get to play? If I liked sitting through lectures I'd be better at school.*

"You will be accompanied by Spec," the Game Runner was saying, "an NPC who can relay information about your surroundings and give advice. Do you know what an NPC is?"

"Yeah, a non-player character," the gamer answered. "But I don't like helpers in a game. Can I disable it?"

The Game Runner frowned for a moment. "I'm afraid that's not an option."

"Those characters always annoy me," the gamer complained. "They pop up every five seconds and tell you what to do. Like it's not obvious."

The Game Runner bristled. "You're here to beta-test the game, not review it," he said sternly. "Now, why don't you pick your gamertag?"

"Solo_Lobo," the gamer answered immediately, crossing his arms. "Solo, underscore, Lobo."

"*Solo lobo*," the Game Runner repeated back in a suddenly computerized voice. "Spanish translation for 'single wolf.'"

"What?" the gamer said with a frown. "No—it was supposed to be 'lone wolf' . . . Ugh, never mind. It's close enough."

The Game Runner stared at him with a blank face, and for a moment the gamer wondered if this guy was an NPC himself.

"Very well," the Game Runner said eventually. "Do you want me to repeat any part of my instructions? Do you understand your objective?"

"Sure. Pop some aliens and escape the station." *One thing I can do is fake like I've been paying attention*, he thought. *Learned that from years of school.*

The Game Runner added, "There are alien guards throughout the game, and if you are careless they will capture you. The third time you are captured, you will fail in your mission and be a permanent prisoner in this world. Do you still accept the assignment?"

"Yep," he said.

"*Buena suerte, Señor Lobo.*" The Game Runner waved a hand and the gamer was plunged into darkness.

Lobo saw lit-up graphics to his left and right. The one on the left said PROLOGUE and the one on the right said PLAY GAME.

It was an easy choice. *I hate sitting through prologues. I want to play a game, not watch a movie.*

He moved toward the PLAY GAME sign.

LEVEL 1

CHAPTER 2

"Wake up, Solo_Lobo."

Lobo's eyes popped open. He was lying on a strange cot. It was shaped like a kite, and his arms and legs dangled to the floor. He got up in a flash and saw that he was wearing a light blue jumpsuit that looked like a prison uniform with his gamertag stitched on the chest. He was in a small oval room with light brown walls. There was no furniture other than the cot. And the room had no edges—the floors curved to connect with the walls and the walls with the ceiling.

"You should exit immediately," the voice said. Lobo wheeled around and saw a softball-sized metal sphere hovering over the bed, waving four robotic arms that were spaced evenly around the sphere. It had a single unblinking lens that telescoped in on him.

"What are you?" he asked.

"My name is Spec," the metal ball said in a female voice that was surprisingly natural-sounding. "I am supposed to guard you, but I want to help you escape."

"Oh, right," he said. *So you're the sidekick.*

"It is critical that you exit this room immediately," she repeated. "An Orionan soldier will enter in precisely fifty-five seconds. Fifty-four seconds. Fifty-three seconds . . ."

"Got it." He opened the door and crept out, passing through a short hallway into a bigger den-like room.

Inside he saw something he figured was a desk—tall, with a top shaped like kidney bean. There was a narrow, rounded cabinet and a funnel-shaped canister on the floor. The furniture was all the same sandy color.

I wasn't put in a prison cell. More like a big closet next to an office. I wonder why?

That probably made it a lot easier to escape.

He opened one of the desk drawers and found it empty.

"I suggest taking a moment to search the premises for useful items and information," Spec said.

"Already doing that," Lobo said. *Here we go with the obvious hints.*

He quickly searched the other drawers. In one he found a digital tablet. When he pushed the tablet's main button, the device opened to a screen with a map of the ship. In one corner of the ship, he saw a pulsing green square inside an oval.

That must be me, he figured. *And the oval is this room.*

He could see the connecting room and a few others, but the rest of the map was grayed out with no details.

"This map isn't complete yet," he said. "Is that part of the game?"

"Game?" the robot echoed.

Of course she wouldn't know this is a game, he realized. "I mean, the first thing I want to do is complete the map."

"You can find detailed information about the entire space station at a data port," the robot told him.

"Got it."

"I suggest exploring the area until you find a data port," she added.

"Already connected those dots," Lobo sighed, rolling his eyes. *This is why I hate game aides. They give me hints I don't need.*

He heard footsteps just outside the door. Spec started to tell him to hide, but he'd already ducked out of the way. An alien entered. It looked sort of like a human but had a wide waist and no shoulders, spindly legs, long arms, and a football-shaped head. Large black oval eyes and flat nostrils sat high on its face, which was tinted with blue-green skin. Its mouth was wide and frowning. It carried a mustard-colored object in one hand.

That sure doesn't look like a weapon, Lobo thought. *Looks more like a big, metallic egg. But who knows? It's alien tech.*

The alien—which Lobo figured was an Orionan—was much taller than Lobo but also looked lightweight and weak. Lobo noticed the door the alien had come through was closed. If he was quick, he could tackle the alien and nobody would see or hear anything. He could probably knock the creature flat and disarm it before it could use that weapon. Then *he* would have a weapon.

He leaped from behind the desk, meaning to tackle the Orionan, but the alien looked at him with eyes that were now glowing. Lobo froze, unable to move. He stood helplessly, mid-step, until darkness overtook him.

CHAPTER 3

Again he found himself in the blackness with the two graphics: PROLOGUE and PLAY GAME.

What just happened? he wondered. *Was that a glitch in the game? Or did I just mess up? Does that count as one of my lives?*

Once again he chose to play the game over watching the prologue.

"Wake up, Solo_Lobo." Lobo opened his eyes. He was back in the kite-shaped bed, which he now realized was made to fit the Orionans' bodies. He stood up. Spec hovered over his head, gesturing with two of her arms.

"What just happened?" he asked.

"The Orionans have powerful lasers in their eyes. They can drain your life force."

"My life force?" he questioned. "Oh!" *They must be disanimators—as soon as they see me, I fade away and go back to Start.* He'd played other games where being caught by an enemy caused the player to disappear, pixel by pixel, until they were sent back to Start. But he'd never experienced it in a virtual reality game before.

"You cannot let them see you for even a moment. If you do, you will be frozen and returned here."

"Why didn't you tell me that before?"

"I assumed you knew," Spec said. "Surely you did not enter the Orionan Cluster without researching their abilities."

"Of course not," he lied. *Did the Game Runner tell me about that? Guess I should have paid more attention.*

"I suggest that you stay out of the sight lines of any aliens," Spec continued.

"You think?" he said sarcastically. Reaching into his pocket, he found that he no longer had the mapping device. He slipped out of the room, headed to the small office, and started searching the drawers again. Empty. "What happened to the map thingy?"

"The alien who caught you kept it."

Lobo turned away from the drawers. "Really? They don't do a complete reboot?"

"Reboot? I do not understand."

"Reboot," he explained. "You know, like resetting things when I go back to the beginning of a level."

Spec took a moment before responding, as if she were struggling to compute. "You mean the entrance to this tier of the space station?"

She doesn't know she's in a game, so she doesn't know what I'm talking about, he reminded himself. "Never mind. I need that map to find my way around."

"I hope you will show more caution," the robot said, and by the tone of her voice it sounded like she meant it. "As an Orionan servant, I have taken a big risk in helping you escape. A failure on your part will have severe consequences for me as well."

"Consequences?" Lobo questioned. "You're

an appliance. What are they going to do—recycle you for parts?"

Spec didn't respond. Lobo felt himself wince a bit, looking away from her. *I guess that was a little harsh. But it's not like she has feelings I can hurt.*

There was a noise at the door. He crouched behind the desk. His hand brushed the floor and hit something hard that scraped across the floor.

He peered beneath the desk to see what it was, hoping it might be loot or some sort of tool he could use. But no, it was useless. A hardened lump of what looked like dried cat food in the shape of a biscuit. A hard biscuit.

It must be Orionan food. Disgusting. Glad this virtual reality doesn't include smells.

The alien entered, looked around for a few seconds, then turned and exited.

Lobo slipped the alien biscuit in his pocket, just in case. *I might have to knock an alien in the head*, he figured. *From behind, obviously. This'll have to do until I get a real weapon.*

He started for the door, but Spec rushed in

front of him and blocked his path. "The area outside this room is well guarded," she said. "There is risk of being seen the moment you leave the room."

"So what do I do?"

"I suggest you observe the aliens and memorize their patterns," the robot said. "That way you can avoid being seen."

"Yeah," he said. "But how am I supposed to learn their patterns if I can't open the door to watch them?"

"Remember that I am an Orionan robot."

"So?"

"The Orionans are used to seeing me. I am as invisible to them as . . . as an appliance, like you said. I can exit the room and observe their patterns, then return with information about their movements."

"Oh!" *So you do serve a purpose. You're a spy!*

"Thanks. Yeah, let's do that."

Spec slipped through the door and was back a moment later.

"Wait . . ." she said. "Wait . . . Wait . . . Wait . . . Go now! Five, four . . ."

Lobo bolted out of the room into a wide hallway. He ducked behind a post just as an alien turned to face the door. The post was wide at the floor and ceiling, but narrowed in the middle. He wasn't hidden very well but the aliens kept their gaze straight ahead.

They act the way teachers tell me to, he thought. *Eyes forward, focus on what's right in front of me, don't pay attention to anything else.*

This hallway was wide in the middle, narrowing at either end, with doors along the curved walls. The walls were mustard yellow and the posts were dark brown.

There was a guard marching along either wall. A third guard entered one room after another, disappearing for a moment, then emerging and moving on to the next door. That was the guard who'd caught him. Lobo could even see the mapping device in the alien's rear pocket. The guard still held the egg-shaped object in its hand.

No way I'm getting that weapon, he thought. *But maybe I can get the map back.*

Lobo moved slowly around the post,

keeping it between him and the guard.

As the guard passed by, Lobo snatched the mapping device out of the alien's pocket. He quickly ducked back behind the post. The alien didn't even notice.

Spec had been hovering by the door, watching. She now zoomed over and he expected her to scold him for being reckless. But he was wrong.

"Excellent work," she said in a low voice.

Lobo stayed hidden behind the post and studied the map. This part of the station was shown on the map. But there was no clue to what was in the other rooms. There would probably be loot in at least one of them. A laser blaster, maybe, or a key he could use somewhere else?

He turned to Spec. "I'm going to check out those rooms."

"I do not recommend it," the robot said. "The doors will be locked."

"But you can open, them right? You could see what's in there."

"I might attract attention if I start barging

into rooms where I am not assigned."

"You *did* tell me to explore," he reminded her.

"You have the entire space station to explore," the robot argued. "I suggest going toward the transport network access portal." She pointed with one of her arms. "From there you can find a data center to complete your map."

"Sounds like a good plan," he admitted. *I wish I knew what I might be missing out on here, but maybe I can come back later.*

He darted from post to post until he reached a narrow opening. Spec stayed close to him. Two guards stood, unmoving, at either side of the opening. There was no way past them without being seen.

"So what's next?" he whispered to Spec.

"We are approaching an aerovator dock," she said. Before he could ask what that was, she went on, "Aerovators are the station's transport network. We can use the capsules to move quickly about the space station."

"But I have to get past those guards."

"Perhaps you can create a distraction."

From down the hall they heard the chatter of alien language.

"Be quick," Spec told him. "They must have noticed you're missing."

Lobo remembered the lump of hard food in his pocket. He reached for it and hurled the lump of stale food at a light hanging from the ceiling. He'd only been hoping to rattle it and distract the guards, but the biscuit actually cracked the fixture.

Oops.

The light dimmed and started spraying sparks. The guards looked up at it and walked closer, staring and speaking rapidly in their language. Lobo darted behind one of them and sprinted down the hall.

As he did words flashed in front of him:

FIRST ACHIEVEMENT UNLOCKED:
ESCAPED LOCKUP

LEVEL 2

CHAPTER 4

Past the opening was a ramp spiraling around to a lower floor. Lobo pressed against the inside wall and peered around the edge. There was the aerovator dock Spec had told him about: an area with four sets of yellow doors that whooshed open and closed to reveal individual capsules. There were clear panes above the doors, looking out into space. He could see the capsules being whisked off through tubes to other parts of the station.

So they're like elevators, he realized, *but they don't just go up and down. They go every direction. Why don't real buildings have those?*

Aliens marched out of one set of doors,

turned, and entered another. They didn't glance at phones or make small talk. They always stared straight ahead and marched promptly to their capsules when it was time.

You have cool stuff, but your lives seem pretty boring, he thought. *Or maybe I'm just saying that because I can't seem to go anywhere without being sidetracked.*

Past the aerovator tubes he could see an entire side of the space station. It looked like a city block of tall buildings wrapped around a sphere. How much of it would he explore in this game?

"This is cool," he whispered to Spec. "I've always wanted to live on a space station."

"Solo_Lobo, you *do* live on a space station. Even before you were captured. An Earth outpost three light-days away."

"Oh. Right." *I forgot I'm not a high school kid to her—I'm a space explorer.* "I meant a space station like this one. It's amazing."

"Indeed," she agreed. "Our progress in space colonization is far ahead of yours. But you should get back to the task at hand and find a data port."

'Back to the task at hand' . . . *Maybe she doesn't know I'm a student, but she sure sounds like a teacher.*

He studied the display over the doors. There were rows of cryptic symbols, lighting up and going dark again. He could see which symbols lit up just before a capsule arrived and which lit up just after they zoomed off. He guessed they showed the departure point and destination of each capsule, like floor numbers over an elevator.

There was a rare moment where the dock was empty. An aerovator chimed. Lobo sprinted for the door. Spec yelled something and hurried after him. The door started to open on a capsule full of Orionans.

Lobo flattened his body next to the doorway. As the aliens stepped out, he slipped behind them and into the capsule. Spec flew in as the doors closed.

"That was risky," she said.

"I knew they wouldn't see me."

"It *was* impressive," she admitted. "How did you know you would not be seen?"

"Have you noticed those guys are always looking straight ahead? They're like robots— um, you know what I mean. As long as I don't get in front of them or make a noise, they don't notice me."

"I see," Spec said, clearly ignoring his remark about robots. "Next time you make a quick decision, it would help if you warn me."

"Got it."

"Now, in order to understand the aerovator transport system, I suggest—"

Lobo pushed a button and the aerovator car started to move.

"I was not going to suggest pushing buttons at random."

"It's not random," he said. "I watched the display. Whatever this symbol is—the three vertical lines—nobody ever came from there or went there. So it must be deserted."

"Also consider the possibility—" Spec started to say, but the capsule lurched as it kicked into high speed. The jolt flung the robot through the air. She made a series of surprised bleeps. A few seconds later, the capsule slowed, and the doors opened on an empty hallway.

"Are you all right?" Lobo asked Spec.

"Yes. I should have anchored myself," she answered. "I rarely use this transport system and forgot the dangers."

"It sure got us here fast, though," Lobo said, peering out into the hall. "And see? I was right. Nobody around." He stepped out of the car and immediately set off an alarm. Red and yellow lights flashed and a siren wailed.

"I was going to suggest that the less-visited areas might be high-security zones," Spec blared over the noise.

"Yeah, thanks!" he shouted back. "Are you good for anything?"

The robot answered by humming noisily. A moment later the sirens quieted and the lights stopped flashing.

"I am good for *that*," she said. "I can talk to the alarm system using sonic signals. I told it that the alarm was falsely triggered. I also opened the door at the end of the hallway."

"Oh. Thanks."

"However, they will send someone to check on the disturbance," she said.

"All right." He started down the hall. Like everything else he'd seen, it was a sandy brown color with rounded walls. "Hey, I didn't mean that about not being good for anything. Actually, you've been pretty helpful."

"Appliances do tend to be helpful," the robot said, hovering beside him as he walked.

"Yeah. Sorry about that crack too." *Why am I apologizing to an NPC—and a robot to boot?*

"It is not accurate to call me an appliance, since I am not designed for specific tasks."

I said I was sorry. Sheesh.

They entered a large room lined with shelves. They were filled with canister-shaped cases, each labeled in alien writing.

"What is this place?" Lobo asked.

"Perhaps you should have determined that before taking us here," Spec said. He didn't think he was imagining the sarcasm in her voice.

He couldn't hold back a small smile. "I hear you. I just wanted to go somewhere that wasn't packed with aliens."

He took a step and almost touched one of the cases, then remembered the alarm. He didn't want to set it off again.

"To answer your question," Spec said, "this is a storage facility for processing cores from failed robots."

"Like a library?"

"More like what you would call a morgue," Spec said.

He turned to her in confusion. "Huh?"

"Your instincts were correct in one way, however; this is a data center, so I can complete your map. I just need to talk to the database." Spec made a humming noise, mixed in with beeps and whistles. "Or at least I can *almost* complete your map."

"Almost?" He stepped out of the doorway and stood between two shelves to stay hidden, just in case. Looking at the map screen, he saw that a lot of the space station was now diagrammed in detail. But big patches of it were unlabeled. The parts that were labeled were done in alien code. He saw they were now at the very tip of one the station's longest branches, far away from everything.

"Can you tell me where I can get a ship out of here?" He studied the map. It showed neon blue lines connecting different parts of the station, which he guessed were aerovator routes. There were a dozen places he could go from this area.

"The Orionan ships are closely guarded and take training to pilot. However, you may be able to send signals from the control room. The Orionans have received your signals for a long time. That's how I was able to learn your language."

He looked up. "What do you mean, send signals?"

"Arrange for a rescue. There is a loading bay where a craft can dock and get us without being detected."

Us? He raised his eyebrows. *I guess she's planning on coming with me, if I get out of here.*

"Is that control room marked on the map? I don't read Orionan."

"Unfortunately, no. It is a secure area and requires additional clearance."

"Well, in that case, at least I know I need to move toward one of the unlabeled areas."

He heard a chime down the hall and quickly looked around the room. "Um, is there any other way out of here?"

"There is not," Spec answered. Footsteps sounded from the hallway outside. "As I warned, there seem to be Orionan soldiers coming to investigate."

CHAPTER 5

Lobo shoved one of the shelves to the ground. As it crashed, he darted to the wall beside the door. The aliens ran into the room, going straight to the wreckage.

Lobo looked up and saw Spec floating in circles over their heads and letting out a high-pitched whirring sound.

What's wrong with her? he wondered. *Is she malfunctioning?*

He gestured to her with his head that he was leaving and then slipped out of the room. He sprinted down the hall and punched the button for the aerovator. The door opened immediately.

Glad it's still here, or we'd be doomed. Wait, what happened to the robot?

He looked back over his shoulder. Spec was just now leaving the room. *Take your time. No need to hurry. No, really.*

Spec cruised down the hall, and they both entered the capsule.

"I could've left without you, but I decided to wait," he felt the need to point out, pushing the button to close the doors. Spec didn't let out a single bleep.

"What's the matter with you?" he asked.

Still nothing.

"That's fine. Be that way."

"Why did you tip the shelf at the data center?" Spec finally asked.

"To win the game."

"What game?"

"I mean, to distract those aliens and get out of there alive," he said. *When I will remember this robot doesn't know we're in a game?*

"The station will now be on high alert. And they know where we are."

"Good point, but I didn't see any other

way out of there."

The robot went back to giving him the silent treatment.

"You know, you're pretty moody for a flying toaster," he muttered. "So where should we go? Any hints?"

The robot let out a series of beeps. He heard alien voices and footsteps just outside the aerovator.

"What are you doing?" he asked Spec.

"I was talking to the aerovator," she explained.

"Nice time for a chat."

"I was learning its route. Your map now shows all of the aerovator routes so you can get around. I also told it not to open the door if there were Orionans outside."

"Oh. Awesome . . . thanks." He glanced at the device, searching for a new location to go to, before hitting a button in the aerovator that matched the symbol on the screen. "Don't forget to anchor yourself." The robot attached one of her arms to the wall just before the capsule shot off like a rocket.

"Thank you," she said.

"No problem."

The aerovator capsule arrived at the new dock. The doors chimed and opened. Words appeared again:

SECOND ACHIEVEMENT UNLOCKED:
REACHED ASTRAL OBSERVATORY

If it wasn't for those alerts, I'd forget I was in a game, he thought. *If I'm in here much longer, I might start taking this as seriously as Spec.* But he could be trapped in this virtual world forever, so maybe it didn't matter anyway.

Then he stepped out and saw the most astounding scene of his life.

LEVEL 3

CHAPTER 6

They were in an observatory, similar to where he first entered the game. But this view surpassed even that one. It seemed like he could see farther into the depths of space than before, and the stars were clearer.

It looks like they're really out there, he thought. *Not just a background graphic.*

But the stars were only part of what amazed him. In the distance were more space stations, bigger than this one, connected by networks of tubes and tunnels. It looked like an entire city floating in outer space. It would take months to explore it all. Maybe years.

But is it really there? Is it part of the game?

There might be more missions to complete.

Spec cruised over from the aerovator dock. "We don't have time to admire the view."

Story of my life, he thought. "Have you ever been out of this station?"

"Of course," Spec said. "I was *designed* for exploration and reconnaissance."

"That's cool." *But that doesn't prove it's real. You're just reciting a scripted backstory.* "I wish I could see the rest of it."

"We need to get out of here first," Spec reminded him.

"I know."

But it was already too late. Another chime sounded from the aerovator dock. He glanced up and saw a set of doors hissing open.

No place to run. Is there a place to hide?

He saw a garbage can—at least he guessed that's what it was. It was like a giant vase, skinny at the base and flared at the top. He dove for it, but it was too narrow to conceal him from the Orionans. Alien guards poured out of the aerovator capsule, and a moment later he was frozen.

CHAPTER 7

I did spend too much time staring out the window, he thought as he plunged back into the darkness.

That's why I'm a bad student. There are too many interesting things outside the window. My mind wanders during tests; my classes don't interest me. But now I'm barely passing high school and have no idea what I'll do with my life.

In the darkness, he saw the same two glowing signs: PLAY GAME and PROLOGUE.

This was his last chance to win the game. *Guess it's time to find out what's in the prologue.* He swam toward the sign.

A scene started to play like a short movie.

He no longer had control over his own actions or motions. *This is why I hate cut scenes*, he thought, *but this is my last life. I don't care so much about being trapped here, but I'm not losing the game without putting up a fight. I'd better find out as much as I can.*

First he saw a space station. It was small and shabby compared to the Orionan ship. There was an image of Earth painted across its broad, silver surface. But he wasn't on the space station. He was drifting away from it, standing at the window of a little ship. *I'm leaving the station*, he realized. *Heading out to explore space.*

He turned and faced people he assumed were his crewmates. Their names appeared over their heads like TV credits, then faded: Jalea, a serious-looking woman with hair cropped close to her head, stood by the ship door. Boris, who wore glasses and looked barely older than Lobo in real life, was next to her. At the ship's controls were Dagney, a very tall, muscular woman, and Chen, a short, stocky man with dark stubble covering most of his face. There was barely enough room for all of them in the tight cockpit.

Jalea was explaining that their mission was to travel through a cloud of space dust and see what was beyond it. Light and sound could not travel through the cloud, so whatever was beyond it was a total mystery to their station's researchers. The ship would not be able to communicate with the space station once it was immersed in the cloud.

"How long will we be out of touch?" Chen asked uneasily.

"However long it takes to complete our mission," Jalea answered.

She continued, telling them all about rumors of an intelligent life-form just beyond the dust cloud. She pulled up holographic slides with bad three-dimensional drawings of Orionans.

Lobo found his mind wandering, then shook his head to bring back his focus. *This is important*, he told himself. *Pay attention.*

Chen leaned forward in his seat. "Where did we get the drawings?"

"From the last scout to enter the cloud," Jalea answered.

"And what happened to him?" Dagney wondered.

Jalea was quiet for a moment, glancing away from them. "We don't know."

The ship jolted to a stop. The light-up displays dimmed and went black. The lights flickered. Dagney turned her attention to the controls, flipping switches and pounding on buttons.

Then the robots broke into the ship. They looked like Spec—little mechanical balls floating in the air, each with four arms. But these robots had laser blasters poking out of their round bodies. Jalea turned to face one and got blasted. She fell to the ground, unconscious.

Lobo tried to bat the robot closest to him out of the air with a fire extinguisher, but the robot turned to him and fired its blaster again. Several aliens pulled Lobo and the other humans out of the ship, and then took them to the cargo bay of a much bigger ship. Lobo saw that their tiny ship had been swallowed whole by the bigger one. The humans were crated like animals and stowed. He could see some of his companions through the slats in his crate: Jalea shouting in frustration; Chen with his hands around his legs, face buried in his knees; Boris examining his cage, as if looking for a way out. Two aliens communicated in hisses and squeals, and they both walked away.

Lobo looked up through the crate and saw a hovering robot watching them. It looked exactly like Spec.

CHAPTER 8

Lobo opened his eyes and found himself back in the cell—he was back at the beginning of the game.

I'm not just supposed to escape, he realized as he stood up. *I'm supposed to rescue my crew. I'm on my last life, and this game is five times harder than I thought it was.*

But Spec wasn't there to help him. The door was locked. He tried it again and again. It didn't budge.

He groaned. *What am I supposed to do? There's nothing useful in here. No cracks in the wall that might be opened. Nothing on the floor to move and reveal a tunnel. No place for a key to be hidden.*

He sat down on the oddly-shaped bed. *Spec let me out the first two times. Did she give up on helping me out of here this time?*

Another thought troubled him: *Was Spec one of the robots that captured me in the first place? They must have hundreds that look exactly the same, but somehow that one seemed more familiar.*

There was a click at the door. He jumped up, half-expecting an alien to enter, but it was Spec.

"There you are!" he shouted, forgetting that he should probably keep his voice down.

Spec floated over to him. "They wanted to know why I was across the station with an escaped prisoner. It took me a while to explain."

"What did you say?"

"I told them you had escaped on your own and I was tracking you," Spec explained. "I said I had just caught up with you when they barged in."

"They believed you, huh? Good job." *I didn't know robots could lie, but I'm glad you're all right.* He hurried past her into the next room.

"No," Spec said, following. "They reassigned me to a different zone, but I slipped away and came back here. And they assigned a new guard to this room." Lobo saw another robot like Spec lying on the floor. "I had to . . . take care of my replacement," she explained.

"So, you have a laser blaster?" *She must. Even if she wasn't the one to capture me, she's that model of robot.*

"Of course. I am a military robot."

"You're going to be in trouble with your bosses," he said.

"Only if they catch me. But they will not, because the two of us are going straight to the control room to call up someone from your space station to come get us."

"We can't. I mean, not right away. I've been playing the game wrong."

"Playing?" Spec said in confusion. "Game? You keep saying that."

"I mean, uh, I just remembered my crew was taken too. I should rescue them from the clutches of these snake-faced dudes."

"We need to escape as soon as we can," Spec argued. "If we get caught . . ."

"I know, but I have to do this," he said. *There's no way I can beat the game without rescuing my crew.* "Can you let me know when it's safe to leave this room? Like you did last time?"

"Yes." Spec ducked out the room and returned a moment later.

"Leave now! Five, four, three . . ."

"Stay close." He bolted out and crouched behind a post. Spec zoomed behind him a moment later.

"I need to check these other rooms," he whispered to her. "In case members of my crew are in any of them."

"It is too risky. We should find the control room and arrange our escape," Spec insisted.

"I can't leave my team behind!"

"I am taking big risks to help you," Spec told him. "If I am caught with you a second time, they will not simply ask questions."

"What'll they do?" Lobo put a finger to his temple. "Can they port in and suck your memory?"

"Yes," Spec said. "And then they would remove my processing core and put it in permanent storage."

Lobo pictured his brain in a jar, like in a sci-fi movie. "That does sound rough," he admitted. "You don't have to take that risk to help me."

"I am not doing it for you," Spec reminded him. "I am doing it so I can escape too. Besides, I have already exposed myself. My only chance now is to leave with you."

"I get it." *So I have to rescue you too? Why don't I just save the entire galaxy while I'm at it?*

"Anyway, I can tell you that your crew members are not in the nearby rooms. We separated you and the other team leader. We kept you far from the others so you couldn't plan an escape together."

"Because you were one of the robots that captured us," he said. *I need to know for sure.*

"Yes. And it was my idea to keep you from the others so you couldn't plan together. But my real purpose was to get you to a less-secure area so we could escape together."

"Are you sure that none of my team are in these other rooms?"

"Yes."

But now I don't know if I can trust you. You didn't tell me about the others. You didn't tell me you helped kidnap me.

"I'm going to check them anyway," he decided.

"You might walk in on an Orionan and get disanimated. And if you get caught again, you may never escape."

"It's a chance I have to take," he said.

The robot made a groaning noise.

Lobo's eyebrows shot up in surprise. *That wasn't some sonic signal*, he thought. *She really is groaning. Can robots get annoyed?*

"I just unlocked all the doors," said Spec.

Oh. Guess I was wrong. She wasn't complaining. She was helping.

As before, there were guards marching back and forth along either side of the hall. A third guard entered and exited each of the four rooms. That one still had the egg-shaped object in its hand.

Lobo entered a room immediately after that guard left. It was filled with cabinets, but nothing of interest was in them. As he slipped out, he narrowly missed walking into the guard patrolling that hallway.

"I told you," Spec hissed. "This is unnecessarily risky."

Lobo grunted and hurried into the next room. The guard checking rooms was now at the other end of the hall.

He found a high table and what looked like food vending machines—those same hard biscuits were in there too. This must have been some kind of alien break room. He shook the machine and something clattered in a small slot. Reaching into the slot, he found a flat, rounded rectangle. He guessed it was an Orionan coin. He plugged it into the machine and bought a biscuit. Two fell.

"Are you going to have a snack?" Spec asked in disbelief.

"I'm not going to eat this garbage. But it's the closest thing I have to a weapon."

He put the biscuits in his pocket and

slipped out again. This time he got lucky. The guard patrolling this side of the room had its back turned.

There was only one more room to check, directly across the hall. He sprinted across and entered. The patrol guard was standing with its back to the door, but as Lobo entered it wheeled around.

CHAPTER 9

There was a zapping sound, and the alien collapsed to the floor.

Lobo glanced over his shoulder to see Spec hovering behind him. A panel on her front had slid open, and the barrel of her laser blaster was sticking out.

"I told you there were no prisoners in these rooms," she said. "Now we have to leave before the other guards raise the alarm."

"Hold on a sec." Lobo searched the guard's unconscious body. He took the egg shaped tool from its hand.

"Is this some kind of a weapon?"

"No. It is a master key. It opens doors using

sonic signals that are outside of your human hearing range."

"I get it now." The creature kept checking on locked rooms. That's why it always had this thing out. *Very useful*, he thought, and put it in his pocket.

"Solo_Lobo," Spec said impatiently.

"I know, I know. We have to get out of here." He stood up and cracked the door, peered out, then ran and ducked behind a post. He zipped from post to post as he had before, Spec staying right behind him.

The guard coming down the hall noticed the open door and walked over to investigate. It peered inside and made a low squeaky noise. The other guard stopped and looked.

With both of the remaining aliens distracted and looking away from him, Lobo sprinted past them into the hallway. He saw the light he'd shattered earlier. It left a narrow path of darkness for him to sneak past the two guards. He reached the aerovator dock, which was empty. Behind him were squeals of alien chatter and footsteps.

He anxiously pressed at the call button and entered the first set of doors that opened. Spec slipped in behind him.

"I suggest—" she started, but he'd already punched the button for the observatory.

"Remember that was where you got trapped."

"I haven't forgotten."

"And since they now know you escaped, they are likely to send guards there at once."

"Then we'll have to beat them there. Anchor yourself."

It was too late. The aerovator capsule kicked into high speed, and Spec whipped across and smacked against the rear wall. "I hate these things," she said.

"I didn't know robots could hate things."

If Spec could glare, he was sure she would right now. But she did chirp a few annoyed beeps at him. "I have a highly-evolved cybernetic intelligence, capable of thoughts and feelings."

"Gotcha," he said.

The car arrived at the observatory.

Lobo stood to the side, watched as the door opened to make sure the coast was clear, and then exited the aerovator capsule. He went straight to the puny trashcan he'd tried to hide behind earlier. He kicked it over, spilling a mysterious pile of contents.

"What are you doing?"

"Getting this!" Grinning, he held up the mapping device. "I hid it just before those alien guys got off the aerovator." He tapped the screen. "The whole map is still here."

I'm back where I left off, but still have a lot to do, he thought. *And I only have one life to do it with.*

"Your decision to come here did give us a tactical advantage," the robot admitted.

"On Earth we say, 'You were right and I was wrong.'"

She made that groaning sound again. This time there were no doors to unlock.

"Let's go," he said, walking toward the aerovators. But one of the doors chimed before they got there.

"Not again!" Spec said.

Lobo remembered the biscuits. He reached into his pocket, grabbed one, and hurled it straight up with all his might, taking out another ceiling light in a flash. The doors hissed open. He stormed into the darkness, crashing into aliens on their way out of the aerovator car. He shoved them aside, stepped into the capsule, and pushed the button to close the door. Spec zipped in just before the door closed.

"Seems like those disanimators don't work in the dark," he said.

"A fortunate discovery," Spec agreed. "But the station will now be on high alert."

"Hey, you're the one who zapped a guy back there."

"Yes, but I would still like to get one step ahead of their guards."

"We are. Where do we go now?"

"Press the yellow button," Spec instructed. Lobo found a big yellow octagon and pushed.

"Hang on," he added, but Spec had remembered this time. The capsule took off, winding through a shaft that curled and curved. At last it arrived with the familiar chime. The doors hissed open, and he was nearly stampeded by a horde of aliens getting in the capsule. He dropped and rolled out of the way.

I would be gone in a heartbeat if those things looked past their own noses. Not that they technically have noses.

He crawled to a small gap between aerovator doors and looked out to see a long corkscrew-shaped ramp, wide as a city block. The ramp was packed with cubbies and kiosks like a hallway in a shopping mall or airport. Here and there were passageways angling off like spokes on a wheel, leading to different parts of the station.

"This is the hub," Spec explained. "You can access most of the space station from here."

"So it's like downtown Alienville," Lobo said. A mass of aliens coursed along, spilling in and out of hallways, pausing at the windows of kiosks, all of them marching forward without dawdling.

Not one guy just hanging out or taking a break,

he noticed. *Is this what humankind will evolve into? A bunch of people so busy doing stuff that they never really do anything?*

"I know at least one of your companions is being held in the storage facility," Spec said. "You can access it one tier up on the opposite side of the hub."

"How am I going to get there? There are a million of these guys walking all over the place. And there's no pattern to how they move."

"The aliens can't see very well in the dark," she reminded him. "Perhaps you can disable the lights to safely make it to the other end of the hallway."

"Good idea." He reached for the last rock-hard biscuit in his pocket and looked up. There were lights all along the ramp.

That's not gonna work, he realized, leaving the biscuit in his pocket. *I'd have to take out a lot of lights. Even if I could do it, I would call a lot of attention to myself.*

"How do I disable the lights?" he asked Spec.

"Be ready to run," the robot answered.

She sailed out into the middle of the ramp. Nobody noticed her at first: just another Orionan robot on an Orionan space station. But then she started to sputter and spin. She hummed and rattled. It sounded like her motor was glitching. Her blaster emerged and fired four times, each taking out a dozen lights and plunging part of the ramp in darkness.

Lobo ran.

CHAPTER 10

Lobo darted to the rear wall, away from the railing. The aliens had all stopped to look at the malfunctioning robot. He jogged behind them with quiet steps.

They're so quiet, he thought. *Shouldn't they be shouting in surprise? Asking each other what's going on? Yelling for help? What's wrong with them?*

He crouched in a corner. An Orionan rolled by on some kind of strange motorized scooter. The deck of the scooter was narrow in the front and wide in the back, and the back was lined with metallic canisters. Then Lobo noticed the scooter was floating a couple of inches above the station floor.

I wish I had a hover scooter. Score another one for alien tech.

After the scooter passed he hurried to the next wing. When he glanced back, he could see the aliens had forgotten the distraction and were moving on. Spec was gone too. He didn't see what had happened to her.

That little robot was brave, he thought. *But there's no way to help her without walking into a nest of aliens, so I'd better focus on rescuing my crew right now.*

He continued down the hallway, darting from post to post. This area didn't seem to have a lot of traffic, and it also didn't seem to be a high-security place like the room he'd trashed earlier. But Spec had told him that at least one of his companions was here, so he was sure he'd run into guards sooner or later.

He came to a gate, which was locked. He pulled the master key from his pocket and waved it. The device made a low humming noise and hissed open. He stepped sideways and peered around the edge. Straight ahead were two guards watching the open gate. They jabbered at each other in their alien language.

They're wondering why the gate opened, he guessed. One of them walked over, stepped through the gate, and looked down the hall, but didn't look his way. The alien walked back in and the gate hissed closed.

It's no use opening the door if I can't get in without being seen, Lobo thought. He put the device back in his pocket. He heard a rumbling behind him and turned. Another alien was rolling up on a delivery scooter. Fortunately the alien was looking back at the crates loaded on the scooter's deck, or Lobo would have been seen and disanimated.

That's right. Spec said this was the storage facility.

The gate hissed open again. The doors opened, and the alien guards waved the scooter in. Lobo had the five seconds he needed to slip inside and hide. He crouched behind a stack of crates and looked around.

Past the guards were towers of crates. Each crate had about twenty sides, like the dice in old role-playing games.

I wonder if they need to guard supplies from other aliens. They seem so well-behaved.

To lift the boxes and stack them onto a tower, the alien on the scooter used a device that had a long bar with a handle on one end and a ring on the other. It looked like the old metal detectors Lobo had once seen in a history lecture.

Lobo tested one of the crates he was hiding behind. He could barely budge it. But the alien was heaving the same-sized crates around easily.

That tool must create a low gravity field around an object so it can be moved. Score a hundred points for alien tech.

The alien finished storing the crates, hung the wand on a rack, and cruised away.

The two guards were patrolling the front of the room, weaving in and out of the crates. And that was the guards he could see—there could be others he couldn't. Lobo reached for a biscuit, thinking he would take out another light, but when he looked up he saw the lights in this room were tucked into the ceiling and protected by thick glass. Instead he climbed a shorter tower of crates. From there he leaped to a higher one, grasping the edge with his fingertips and scrambling up. The guards didn't notice. He reached a third tower by leaping to the side and climbing a post.

From there he could see the entire room. It was shaped like a pentagon, with four walls and the fifth side open to the hallway. There were doors in three of the four walls.

There's a human in at least one of those rooms, he thought. *But which one?*

None of the doors would be easy to get to. One of the guards always seemed to be watching every door. When one turned away from a door, another started marching toward it.

As he scanned the room, Lobo realized the wand's rack was out of sight of the guards. He leaped to the top of another tower, then another. He was as close as he could get to the gravity wand, but it was too far to jump. He would have to drop to the floor and would surely be seen. He glanced up and noticed a dangling chain between him and the tower.

That's good luck, he said to himself. *No—not luck. Design. I'm in a game, and they have to give me a way to win. I'm so into this game that I forget I'm playing one.*

He leaped for the chain, grasped it, and swung over to the post. Still dangling from the chain, he grabbed the wand from its hook and used his feet to kick off the wall and swing back to the crates.

Once he was safely out of sight, he inspected the wand. There was a button on the barrel. He aimed it and pressed the button with his thumb. A tower several feet away shifted. Lobo swung the wand sideways, and the tower's top crate crashed to the floor.

One of the guards paused and said something in alien language. The other guards came to investigate. Lobo leaped to another tower, then scrambled down. He saw a clear path between the towers of crates and one of the doors. He ran over, tucking the gravity wand under his elbow so he could grab his master key and wave it at the door.

The room was the size and shape of the cell

he'd been kept in, but there were no humans here. He groaned. *Come on. Seriously?*

Behind a high, narrow table was a wall panel. He opened it and saw a column of switches. *I wonder what these do. Only one way to find out.*

Lobo went down the row and flipped every switch. The room went black, but he ran his hand down the panel to find and flip more switches until he'd hit them all. He heard more alien voices from the room outside.

He crept out of the room into absolute blackness. Then he made his way along the wall toward the next door. He crashed into an alien, but simply shoved it out of the way.

Can't stun me in the dark, Snake-face.

He found the next room and entered.

"Anyone in here?" he asked the darkness.

"What's going on?" came a woman's voice. "Who's there?"

A human! "It's me, Lobo—er, Solo_Lobo," he said. "Come on, we have to hurry."

"Do I need to remind you who's the leader of this unit?" the woman answered sternly.

Jalea. He remembered the woman from the prologue. *She's my commander. But she's an NPC. I don't really have to take orders from her, just keep her from getting killed.*

"Sorry, Commander, but we really are in a hurry," he said. "Once they get the lights back on we're screwed." He turned back to the door when a light shone in his face. He squinted against it and saw Spec aiming a beam at him.

His eyes focused in the harsh light a bit more, and he could see slight differences in this robot. *No. Not Spec. A robot that looks like Spec.*

A panel opened on its front and a laser blaster emerged.

CHAPTER 11

The robot wavered in the air, widening its beam to cover both him and Jalea. It moved its blaster back and forth to keep aim on both of them. Then it started making a high-pitched noise.

It's calling for help, Lobo guessed. *It doesn't want to kill us, but it needs reinforcements.*

He still had the gravity wand tucked in the crook of his arm. While the robot was looking at Jalea, Lobo shifted the gravity wand and grasped the handle. The robot turned back, its lens telescoping and searching him. He froze in exactly the same posture as before, hoping it wouldn't notice the difference.

"Hey, robot!" Jalea shouted. The robot shifted its attention back to her. With one gesture, Lobo raised the gravity wand and pushed the button on the handle. He grabbed the robot with the wand's force and hurled it as quickly as he could. The sphere crashed against the hard wall and fell to the floor.

"You forgot to anchor yourself," he said.

"Let's go!" Jalea ordered, but Lobo didn't need to be told. He was already kicking the door open and running through the dark along the wall.

"Follow me!" he shouted. "I know the way."

"Remember who's commander here," Jaela snapped, but she did stay with him. Lobo body-checked another guard aside and opened the gate. The light from the hallway spilled into the dark room.

I'm at a high risk for getting disanimated right about now, Lobo realized. He used the wand to toss a nearby crate at the closest tower. The tower toppled, colliding with another tower. That one fell and hit a third. Soon crates were crashing like a row of dominoes. Lobo ran through the hall with Jalea hot on his heels. He waved the key at the first door he saw and ducked inside, pulling Jalea after him. A moment later a troop of aliens stormed by.

He'd almost forgotten about the levels of the game until the familiar words appeared:

THIRD ACHIEVEMENT UNLOCKED:
RESCUED COMMANDER

LEVEL 4

CHAPTER 12

"Good work, Solo_Lobo," Jalea said. Apparently she didn't hear the announcement.

"Thanks. You too. You distracted the robot, and I was able to take it out." He realized the wand had a strap he could pull out, so he used it to drape the wand over one shoulder. It was nice to have his hands free.

"Now we have to find a way off this space station."

"But first we have to find the rest of the crew," he said.

"No," she said. "By now there should be a rescue craft looking for us. If we can let them know our location, we can get out of here within the next hour."

Lobo frowned. "But we can't leave the others behind!"

"Our priority is to relay information to the home base," Jalea said sternly. "The Orionans are planning to invade our star system. I wasn't able to figure out much of their language, but it seems like they're preparing to take our people captive and build their own empire. We must get this information back to our station. Don't you remember the debriefing?"

Not really, he thought. *I tried listening, but . . . it's hard to remember it all.*

"Do you know how we can send a message to our rescue ship?" Jalea asked.

"I know there's a control room," Lobo told her. "They have radio equipment that intercepts our signals. The Orionans have been using it to spy on us. We should be able to use it to send our own messages."

"So take me to this control room," Jalea ordered.

"I don't know where it is. But it must be in one of the gray areas on this map." He pulled out the mapping device.

"Let me see it." His commander held out her hand, and he reluctantly handed it over.

"We have to go to the hub first," Lobo explained, pointing to the map. "That's the big area in the middle."

Jalea stared intently at the map. "It looks like we have to go to this central area to access other parts of the space station." She tapped the screen. "We should go there."

You think? Lobo had to make a real effort to avoid making the comment out loud. Instead, he simply said, "Good idea, Commander."

"In line, Lieutenant Lobo." Jalea marched out of the room, carrying the mapping device. Lobo hurried after her.

Is she going to keep my map? he wondered. *Never mind. At least I still have the gravity wand.*

They hurried down the hallway, staying close to the wall, until they came to the hub. Jalea crouched at the entrance and watched all the activity.

"You can't let any of them see you," Lobo whispered.

"I know that," she said crossly.

But do you know about their disanimating eyes? he wondered.

He looked over her shoulder. "We need to find a way across the hub without being noticed."

Keeping her gaze on the aliens moving through the hub, Jalea snapped, "I'll tell you when I need advice, Lieutenant. For now you can keep silent."

Lobo narrowed his eyes and stepped back. *I miss Spec*, he thought.

One of the cargo scooters rolled by. It was piled with canisters.

"I've got this," he said without explaining or waiting for Jalea's response. He drew his gravity wand and pushed the button, aiming it at the canisters on the rear of the cart. They bounced and rolled down the ramp. Aliens leaped out of the way.

Lobo ran up the ramp toward the next landing. He looked back and saw that Jalea was keeping up with him. She nearly crashed into him as he entered the passageway. "Why did you do that, Lieutenant?" she asked. "I did not give you an order!"

"Sorry, I had to act fast."

"Well, you did get us here," she admitted. She looked at the map. "This area isn't charted. Maybe the control room is here."

"It might be," he agreed, knowing it would be easier to work around her if he let her think she was in charge. *But hopefully we'll find our crewmates before we find the control room.*

The passageway split off into several narrow hallways, making him think of a squid with tentacles. In his mind he named it The Squid.

"I can't read any of this," Jalea muttered to herself, tapping at the map.

Lobo studied the symbols at the beginning of each hall, hoping they might give him a clue to where they led. One symbol was made of two interlocking squares. Another was a triangle on top of a V shape. A third looked like a backward D inside a circle. He had no idea what they might mean.

But humans actually designed this whole space station, he reminded himself, *because this is a game. How can I keep forgetting that? That's never happened to me before.*

But this wasn't the time to reflect on that, and he knew it. He brought his attention back to his mission. *There must be a clue to the correct hall, but what is it? And why does that one with the squares look so familiar?*

"We need to figure out what the symbols mean," he said to Jalea, who was still poking around on the map.

"Thank you, Lieutenant Obvious," she said.

No need to be rude, he thought. Then he felt a pang of guilt as he realized this was exactly how he'd first treated Spec.

But suddenly he noticed: Jalea had the same interlocking squares on her prison jumpsuit! He glanced at his chest and saw that he did as well. If the symbol was on prisoner clothes, the symbol on the wall must point the way to the prison itself. And the rest of the crew would be there. Spec had told him they'd only separated him and Jalea.

That's where we have to go, but Jalea can't know why.

"Let's just take one at a time and see where it goes," he suggested. "Process of elimination. Might as well try this one first."

Jalea opened her mouth. He thought she was going to argue, but no sound came out. She was gazing at something over his head. He turned around and saw one of the hovering robots had appeared behind him.

"I found the control room," the robot said in a familiar voice.

Lobo grinned. "Spec!" Then he felt the gravity wand being pulled off of his shoulder.

"Hey!" he whirled around and saw Jalea aiming the wand at Spec. "She's an ally!" he shouted. "Don't hurt her!"

Spec's blaster emerged from her front panel. She took aim at Jalea.

"Don't shoot!" he shouted at Spec.

Spec fired at the same moment Jalea found the button on the gravity wand and flung Spec toward the wall.

CHAPTER 13

The force of the gravity wand bent the laser beam, keeping it from hitting Jalea. Spec wobbled and flew toward the wall but stopped herself before crashing.

"Spec, put your blaster away," Lobo urged. "Jalea, put the wand down."

Spec let out a low beep and slid the blaster back into its panel. Jalea slowly lowered the gravity wand.

I'm guessing I won't get that back either, Lobo thought, rolling his eyes. He turned back to Spec. "How did you get away?"

"I escaped from the repair facility. But I think it would be wise to get off the station as soon as possible."

"Yes," Jalea agreed. "And you know the way to the control room?"

"It is down this hallway." Spec pointed with one of her arms. "I will lead the way and watch for Orionans."

Jalea gave Lobo a sidelong look. "Are you sure we can trust this thing? What if it leads us right into a nest of aliens?"

Lobo crossed his arms. "If she wanted me captured, she wouldn't have helped me escape in the first place."

Jalea clicked her tongue. She still seemed suspicious.

"You go with her. I'm going to go find the others," Lobo said.

"You are not," Jalea said. "Our mission was to gather as much information as we could. Now that we know the aliens are planning to attack, it's urgent that we return to our station. We should not endanger ourselves further."

"But we can't just leave them here!" Lobo insisted. "If there really is an invasion coming, then our crew will be in danger as hostages."

Jalea narrowed her eyes and squared her shoulders. "Lieutenant, this is a direct order."

"I'll be back ASAP." He started down the hallway with the overlapping squares.

"If you get caught, there will be no rescue," Jalea shouted after him.

"I don't expect one," he called back.

Spec zoomed after him. "I forbid this," she said, opening her front panel and aiming the blaster at him. "Follow your commander's orders and go to the control room."

Lobo froze his steps. *Is this for real? Spec is threatening me?*

"Why are you doing this?" he asked.

"Because my own rescue depends on your cooperation," she said. "You still think I am a friend. I am not. I am merely helping you so I can achieve my own goals. And your rescue plan puts us all at risk."

"That's not true," said Lobo. "You risked yourself back on the hub to save me."

She paused before saying, "I calculated that it was the best risk."

"Come on," he said. "You like me at least a little."

The robot said nothing.

"Don't you have . . . others?" Lobo asked. They didn't have time for this, but he needed to convince her to see things his way. "People . . . I mean, *robots* that you want to rescue? Like, family?"

"I am a robot," she said. "I have a serial number, not a family."

"Friends, then. You said you have a highly-evolved intelligence with thoughts and feelings, so if there are other robots like you, you must have ones you care about."

Finally Spec said, "Yes. There are robots I care about. Most of them are in storage. You dumped some of them on the floor, if you recall."

Lobo felt his stomach drop, remembering the strange way Spec had reacted when he'd tipped that shelf. *That data center—she said it was a storage facility for processing cores. Those canisters were basically the souls of her robot friends.*

"I'm sorry," he said. "I didn't know."

"Never mind. My point is that I am leaving them behind too." Her voice was even. Either Spec was unable to sound sad, or she had an iron will. "It is every bot for itself."

"But you would save them if you could," he pushed. "Right?"

The robot hovered quietly for a moment.

"Right?" Lobo repeated.

"Follow the hallway with the intersecting squares to find your crewmates."

"I already figured that out. But it's nice to have confirmation."

"There is an emergency portal near the control room," Spec continued. "After you get the others, come back and follow the far left hallway all the way to the end. If the rescue ship arrives before you do, we will leave you behind."

"Got it. If I don't win—I mean, if I don't succeed, uh . . . thanks for everything. And good luck."

"Hurry," the robot said, and then flew off down the hallway.

Did I just treat an NPC like a person? Lobo

wondered as he hurried down the hall. *But she does feel like a person. More of a person than a lot of people I know. She's been a better friend to me than most of the people I hang out with.*

In the middle of the hall, he saw a sign with a message in bold alien script. Lobo paused. He had no idea what that could mean. *It probably says "Beware!" Or "Do Not Enter!" Or "Only Authorized Personnel Beyond This Point!"*

From farther down the tunnel he heard a whistling noise. He hid behind the sign as a fleet of hover-scooters sped by. These Orionans were wearing padded outfits that made them look almost—but not quite—like humans. They carried weapons that looked like blasters.

That must be armor, Lobo thought. *They're going into battle. Hope they aren't going to the control room.*

He glanced down the hall again. There were no other places to hide. He would have to make a run for it.

He sprinted down the hallway, which seemed to go on forever. *No wonder they use those scooters. It's a long way to the prison.*

Another whistling noise sounded, meaning another scooter was coming toward him. He glanced back. There was no time to get back to the sign.

They always keep their eyes straight forward, he remembered. He lay on the floor near the wall. The scooter zoomed on with no sign of slowing. As he hoped, the alien kept looking forward without a single sideways glance. Lobo rolled, kicked at the scooter, and sent it crashing into the wall. The alien jolted forward and banged its head, then collapsed on the ground. The scooter bounced back and came to a stop, upright, next to Lobo.

Lobo crouched over the unconscious alien. He removed its helmet and peeled off its armor, placing it on his own body. He expected it to be too long and too tight, but the stretchy armor conformed to his own body.

Another awesome alien technology. One size truly fits all.

The exception was the helmet, which was too big side to side and a tight squeeze front to back, especially on the nose.

It wasn't designed for things with noses, he realized. *At least I can see through these big eyeholes.*

Lobo stepped onto the scooter, glancing down to look at the buttons and a lever. He tapped on a button and the scooter jolted backward.

Okay, that's what that does.

He hit the lever and rotated left. He kept turning until the scooter was facing down the hall, and then tapped a third button hard. The scooter took off like a rocket.

FOURTH ACHIEVEMENT UNLOCKED:
STARTED RESCUE MISSION

LEVEL 5

CHAPTER 14

The hallway was even longer than he expected, twisting and turning for what must have been miles. It passed long series of windows that looked out at the stars or revealed the bigger part of the space station, which was now far away. He had to be careful and use quick reflexes to keep the scooter from crashing, but it was a fun ride.

He passed what looked like security cameras and came to a stop in front of a gate. He waved his key and it opened.

At least Jalea didn't take my key too.

This new space was brightly lit. Guards stood to the left and right of the gate, but he just cruised right by them. They barely acknowledged him.

Glad these guys aren't much for small talk.

The hallway ended at a Y-shaped junction. On the left was a long, low counter. On the right was a tightly guarded gate. In between the two paths was a row of parked scooters. Lobo parked his and glanced at the gate. There were three guards standing in front. He would have to walk by them to unlock the gate.

I don't want to risk it, he thought. *Maybe I can find another way past that gate.*

Behind the counter on the left was a bustling office. He guessed it was some kind of station for the guards. He marched in like he knew exactly where he was going. A dozen aliens were at work. Some talked to each other in low voices, while others looked at monitors and tapped on touch screens.

He made his way through a maze of desks and low walls. At the far end was another guarded door.

I need to look like I know what I'm doing.

He turned around again and saw more egg-shaped devices dangling from hooks.

Key rack, he figured. He took one. *Two birds, one stone. Now that guard knows why I'm here, plus I have another key. It probably works on more doors in this area than the other one.*

The guard said something that sounded like an order or a gruff question. Lobo pretended not to hear and marched back out of the office, resisting the urge to look back. He didn't want to raise any suspicions.

Outside the office area, a couple of armored Orionans pulled up to the gate in a vehicle. It was like a miniature truck, wide enough for a second alien to ride shotgun. That wasn't just an expression—this alien was armed with a blaster.

Keep moving. Look busy, Lobo reminded himself. He strode forward until he was behind the truck. A large orange crate sat on the rear of the vehicle. It was the same shape as the crates in the storage area, but much bigger, with holes along the top.

Air holes, he realized. *Is Jalea in that crate?*

The gate opened, and the guards stood aside to let the truck through.

Here's my chance to get past those guards . . .

He leaped on the back of the truck and hid behind the crate. The truck cruised through the gate and onto a ramp. It was a long corkscrew-style ramp, like the hub, but with lower ceilings and tighter turns. In the middle was a wide post. The outside wall was lined with doors.

Prison cells, he realized. *That's why this place is so tightly guarded.*

He peered into the holes of the crate, half-expecting to see Jalea. Instead he saw something that looked a little like a human but had tusks and matted hair all over its body. It was asleep, but stirring.

All right. Guess they aren't just kidnapping humans. Other life forms are also in trouble. Seems like these guys are making a lot of enemies—could come in handy if we needed some allies.

He leaped off the back of the truck and hid behind the center post. The truck continued on. He followed, staying far enough back to remain hidden. The ramp coiled around ten times, containing about sixty cells.

The truck stopped at the bottom and the alien soldiers jumped off. The driver used a gravity wand to lift the crate from the truck bed, set it on the ground, and then move it along a few feet at a time.

The other soldier watched, holding his blaster ready. *In case that creature breaks out,* Lobo guessed. *Looks like they'll be busy for a few minutes.*

He started up the ramp, whispering at every door, "Anyone in there from Earth?" Creatures grunted, hissed, and growled in reply.

Finally he heard a human respond. "Solo_Lobo? Is that you?"

He didn't quite recognize the voice, but when he opened the door with his key from the guard station, he saw Chen looking at him with wide eyes. Lobo remembered he was wearing the armor of an Orionan guard. He took off his helmet.

"Relax, it's me. Jalea is safe too," he said.

At least I think she is. "Do you know where the others are?"

"No." Chen shook his head. "But we have to find them!"

"Let's check the other cells." *At last, someone who isn't throwing everyone else under the bus.*

They found Dagney a few doors down. "You're alive!" she said to Lobo.

"For now," he said. "Come on!"

The three of them continued. They were nearly to the top when Lobo heard the whistling motor of the truck coming back up the ramp.

"Hide!" He unlocked a door and herded his crewmates into the cell.

"We don't know what's in here!" Chen protested.

"We do know what's back there—the bad guys." He closed the door almost entirely, leaving a thin crack for him to peer through. The truck cruised by without stopping.

Dagney tugged on his sleeve. "We have to get out of here," she whispered.

"Wait." The truck had paused at the top of the ramp. The Orionans were waiting for the gate to open.

"Come on!" Chen hissed.

Lobo looked back into the cell and saw a strange creature. It was shapeless and inky black, with hundreds of eyes floating in its blobby body. Countless tendrils whipped around as it crept toward them.

I'd rather take my chances with the Orionans, he thought. They bolted out of the room, and he cringed as the door slammed behind them.

The gate was open, but the truck hadn't gone out yet. One of the Orionans made a noise, and the truck started to turn around.

CHAPTER 15

"Run!" Lobo shouted, starting down the ramp. Dagney and Chen kept up with him, the three of them bumping elbows as they ran. The truck followed, keeping a slow pace because of the tight turns of the ramp. They managed to stay just far enough ahead to avoid coming into view of the Orionans.

But we'll run out of ramp pretty soon.

They reached the bottom. The Orionans were almost in view behind them.

"Stand back!" Lobo shouted. He waved his key at the last door and threw it open. The hairy, toothy creature from before charged out. It was at least eight feet tall, with long, sharp tusks. It had the large, floppy ears of an elephant, a short trunk, and the powerful body of a gorilla.

Half Bigfoot, half woolly mammoth, Lobo thought. *All angry.*

The creature looked at Dagney and Chen cowering against the wall. Then it saw the Orionan guards. It let out a big, bellowing trumpet noise and charged toward them, obviously considering them to be the greater enemy. The guards couldn't turn the truck around quickly enough, so they leaped off and ran back up the ramp. The elephant-headed creature stomped after them.

"Glad that thing is on our side," Dagney said with a sigh.

"For now," Chen added.

Then they heard a human groan from behind the second-to-last door. Lobo unlocked the door to find Boris hunched against the back wall of cell. Dagney and Chen rushed in to help him up.

"I don't think he can walk," Chen said.

"Take him to the truck," Lobo instructed.

The three of them helped Boris to the truck, shoving the empty crate off the back and lowering him onto it. Chen crouched and held him.

Lobo heard chaos at the top of the ramp: growls and shrieks and stampeding feet. The creature they had released was getting its revenge.

But what about the others in these cells? Lobo wondered. *Are any of them actually criminals? Or did they just get captured, like we did?*

"The lever turns the truck left and right," he told Dagney. "The left button is the brake and reverse; the right button is the accelerator. Drive to the top of the ramp."

"Sure thing," she said. She stood in the driver's perch and stabbed at the accelerator button. The truck lurched forward, jerking everyone in it. Boris groaned and Dagney looked back at him sheepishly. She pressed the accelerator again, this time lightly resting her finger on it. The truck started to cruise.

Lobo ran alongside it, waving his key at every door. One after the other, they clicked open. Prisoners poured out, some running, some crawling, some oozing.

The gate at the top was still open, while several Orionans lay crumpled on the floor. Sirens wailed and lights flashed. Lobo unlocked the last door and leaped into the passenger side of the truck.

"Brake!" he shouted as they reached the guard station. Dagney found the brake button and brought the truck to a stop with a jolt. Lobo leaped off, grabbed a blaster from the counter, and leaped back on.

"That way! Go!" he shouted, pointing to the exit. Dagney turned the truck and headed for the exit. "Do you want to drive or defend?"

"Drive!" she answered. "I'm getting the hang of this thing."

"Good, because the next part is pretty wild!"

Lobo looked back once and caught a final glimpse of the guard station. Something like a chicken crossed with a dinosaur was on the counter. A cow-sized hedgehog was crushing the door. The many-eyed black blob was oozing quietly along, absorbing everything into its body.

The sirens and lights continued in the hallway. Guard bots and armed aliens appeared on the edges, firing lasers at them. Lobo took them out with his blaster while Dagney steered. The stars blurred by as she passed the first set of windows. She took the twists and turns easily, even in the heavy truck. She went faster and faster as the hallway straightened out.

"You're good at this!" Lobo shouted.

"I *am* a professional pilot!" She slowed as they came to passageway he called The Squid.

"That one," he said, pointing out the path Spec said led to the control room and escape port. She sped up again.

FIFTH ACHIEVEMENT UNLOCKED:
RESCUED TEAM

LEVEL 6

CHAPTER 16

He saw Jalea up ahead, waving. She had found a blaster and was guarding the hall. Dagney slowed down.

"There's a docking station at the end!" Jalea shouted. "We took care of the guards and are awaiting rescue."

"What does she mean by *we*?" Dagney asked. "The rest of our crew is right here."

"We made a friend," Lobo explained.

They cruised to the docking bay, a hexagonal tunnel covered with glowing green lights and dark walls. Spec was in the control room in the bay, talking into the radio. Lobo heard human voices report back, as clear as if it came from the next room.

"We're nearly there," said a man's voice over the speaker. "We've identified a blind spot in the alien station's detection system and are traveling through it now."

"Suit up!" Jalea shouted. She pointed her blaster at a rack of space suits designed for Orionan bodies. "Be ready to board ship."

"Those will never fit us," Chen said, frowning.

"They might," Lobo told him. "Try it."

Lobo took off his armor and grabbed one of the alien suits. He dragged the long, skinny pants over his legs. The fabric both shrank and stretched to fit his body. He took Jalea's blaster and his gravity wand and guarded the room so the others could get suited up.

As he waited, he glanced out the portal window and saw stars, planets, and the string of Orionan space stations. *There's so much to discover out there.*

He heard a noise and looked back to the hallway. A mob of robots with laser blasters was coming straight for them.

Should've known we weren't quite done yet.

Lobo slammed the door to the control room closed so the others would be safe. Then he aimed his blaster. He easily took out the first few waves of bots. He'd played a lot of shooter games in his life. The following waves of robots started moving and firing faster. He kept moving and firing with his laser, relieved that Spec was still in the control room and couldn't see him taking out bots. But these robots didn't seem as real or advanced as she was. These were just targets.

In the next wave, Orionans joined the mass of bots. They sped down the hall in trucks, firing lasers. Lobo took out the lights so they couldn't disanimate him. Debris rained down and the lights dimmed.

He switched to the gravity wand and used it to send the trucks rolling toward the bots. It was harder than using the blaster, but by rolling the trucks across the hallway he was able to knock out a row of bots all at once.

At last a new robot appeared, big enough to fill the hallway. Dozens of smaller bots poured out of it. Lobo had to clear out the mini-bots with his blaster, then quickly switch to the gravity wand and throw the giant robot over. After five or six rolls, the machine exploded. More debris rained down from the ceiling.

"The escape ship is here!" Jalea shouted.

That was the final boss, Lobo realized. *Now the game ends. I wish there was one more phase. Or better yet, one more mission.*

He turned to see the Earth ship secured to the portal's hatch. Chen, Boris, and Dagney lowered themselves into the ship. Jalea waved him on.

But he hesitated to follow. "I don't want to go."

"What do you mean?" she shouted.

"There's more to do."

Jalea's face changed. Literally. It *transformed.* He realized he was now talking to the Game Runner.

"You've almost won the game," the Game Runner said.

"I might have won, but I haven't finished. I want to complete all the missions. Plus, I want to see it all." He gestured out the window.

"If you don't leave now, you'll be trapped in the game forever."

"Forever," Lobo echoed. *But I've finally found a real adventure here. I never feel like that in real life.*

"Maybe I'll find my own way out," he added. "I'll find a ship and figure out how to fly it, then search the farthest corners of the game. If I ever want to come back, I'll figure out a way."

"Think about your decision carefully," the Game Runner said.

Lobo squared his shoulders. "You know what? I'm not just here for your convenience. Hear that, L33T C0RP?" He lifted his head, shouting to more than just the Game Runner. "I'm not finished here, and you can't just kick me out."

I want to see this through, he thought, *in a way I've never wanted to finish something before.*

"Spec," he said, turning to her, "Do you want to come with me? We can rescue the others first, and then there's so much more to do. We can help defend Earth's space station against the Orionan invasion, travel the galaxy to find allies . . ."

The robot aimed her telescoping eye at the escape ship, then at him. He could almost hear the motor of her brain as she thought it over. "I don't know, Lobo."

Maybe this was crazy. He was choosing to stay inside a video game that he didn't know if he'd be able to leave again. He was asking a non-player character to go against its program.

But she seems like more than a non-player character, he admitted to himself. *And wait—did she just call me by a nickname? Maybe she's not just an ordinary, programmed NPC . . .*

Still. Was he making the right choice?

Then Spec floated over to him, and he could feel the relief in his chest. He knew what he wanted her answer to be.

"Get us to a ship," Spec said. "We have an invasion to prepare for."

WHAT WOULD YOU DO IF YOU WOKE UP IN A VIDEO GAME?

CHECK OUT ALL OF THE TITLES IN THE

LEVEL UP
SERIES

[ALIEN INVASION] [LABYRINTH] [POD RACER]
[REALM OF MYSTICS] [SAFE ZONE]
[THE ZEPHYR CONSPIRACY]

SOME PLACES HOLD MORE SECRETS THAN PEOPLE.
ENTER AT YOUR OWN RISK.

THE ATLAS OF CURSED PLACES
BREAKDOWN
KATHRYN J. BEHERNS

THE ATLAS OF CURSED PLACES
DEADMAN ANCHOR
N. R. COLEMAN

THE ATLAS OF CURSED PLACES
DIRECTOR'S CUT
VANESSA ACTON

THE ATLAS OF CURSED PLACES
RADIOACTIVE
VANESSA ACTON

THE ATLAS OF CURSED PLACES
SKELETON TOWER
VANESSA ACTON

THE ATLAS OF CURSED PLACES
THE GATEWAY
KATHRYN J. BEHERNS

THE ATLAS OF CURSED PLACES

ABOUT THE AUTHOR

Israel Keats was born and raised in North Dakota and now lives in Minneapolis. He is fond of dogs and national parks. His favorite games include *Portal*, *The Legend of Zelda* series, and *Plants vs. Zombies*. He also loves *Pokémon GO*, since it's the first game he can play while walking his dog.